ISABELLA
AT THE LIBRARY

Written by
Kate Mahoney-Veitch

Illustrated by
Sarah-Leigh Wills

For Laura, for loving me just for being me,
for your honesty, open mind and big heart.
My soul mate and the one and only GG!

ISABELLA AT THE LIBRARY

Illustration and design by Sarah-Leigh Wills.
www.happydesigner.co.uk

Isabella is a little girl who loves soft toys; she has so many of them that they take up most of her bed, the window sills in her bedroom, on top of her wardrobe and bookshelves. She loves them all, but her favourites are Monkey Snuggles, Snuggly Rabbit, Jessie the Cat, Daddy Leopard, Baby Leopard and Duke the Pup.

Isabella also absolutely loves books, she has lots of them; three bookshelves full in fact! She loves looking at the pictures and telling magical stories to her soft toys.

One of Isabella's favourite places to go is the library. She goes twice a week, once for music time and once for stories and crafts. Her Mummy and little brother, Vinnie, always go with her, along with two of her favourite soft toys.

Today Isabella takes Monkey Snuggles and Duke the Pup to the library. After music time she chooses some books, settles down on a bean bag and starts telling a magical story.

"One day, a little girl called Isabella goes to the library with her Mummy, brother, Monkey and Pup."

"Today it is music time. First they sing "Row, Row, Row Your Boat". Isabella has Monkey and Pup in her boat, Mummy has Vinnie in her boat and Lucy the Librarian has a big teddy in her boat. They row and row until they come to a shore. They see a big lion and he makes a big roar. Monkey is a bit scared but Pup gives him a lick."

"They row some more and they come to a stream, where they see crocodile who makes them all scream!"

Aargh!

"Next they sing "Twinkle Twinkle Little Star";
the night sky looks magical with the full
moon and lots of twinkling stars."

"Vinnie almost falls asleep until Duke the Pup starts howling at the moon. He causes such a commotion that Lucy the Librarian really has to shush him!"

"To finish they sing "Round and Round the Garden". Duke the Pup takes Isabella's hand and sings, "Round and round the garden, like a puppy dog; one step, two step, and tickly under there!"

"Pup licks and tickles Isabella, all up her arms, over her tummy and finally under her chin until she falls around laughing."

"Time to go," says Mummy.
Isabella closes her book and gathers her soft toys around her; she gives them a big hug and jumps up. She takes her Mummy's hand, smiles, and says, "I love coming to the library, I can't wait to come back again soon!"

THE ISABELLA SERIES...

Isabella is a little girl who adores soft toys and books. She loves making up magical stories where her soft toys come to life and have exciting adventures with her.

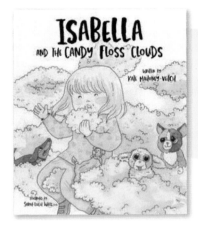

ISABELLA AND THE CANDY FLOSS CLOUDS

In this story Isabella and her soft toys wake up in clouds made of candy floss and discover a sticky world of shapes.

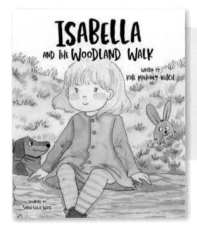

ISABELLA AND THE WOODLAND WALK

In this story Isabella goes for a woodland walk with her soft toys but one of them gets lost!

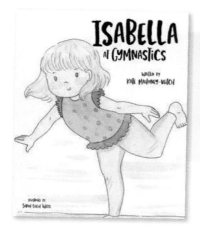

ISABELLA AT GYMNASTICS

In this story Isabella and her soft toys all go to gymnastics and turn a bit wild!

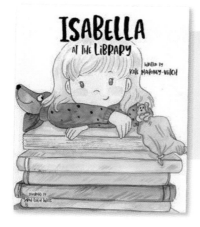

ISABELLA AT THE LIBRARY

In this story Isabella and her soft toys go to the library where they visit the world of nursery rhymes.

ISABELLA AND THE MAGIC UMBRELLA

In this story Isabella and her soft toys discover that they have a magic umbrella.

Printed in Poland
by Amazon Fulfillment
Poland Sp. z o.o., Wrocław